7/98 - 35x - 7/98
9/02 - 53x - 1/02

E   214973

Hennessy, B. G.
School days

SCHOOL DAYS

SCHOOL DAYS

By B.G. Hennessy

Pictures by Tracey Campbell Pearson

Viking

Special thanks to the teachers and children
of Jericho Elementary and Heathcote School.

T.C.P. and B.G.H.

The artwork for each painting consists of an ink,
watercolor, and gouache painting that was camera
separated and reproduced in full color.

VIKING
Published by the Penguin Group
Viking Penguin, a division of Penguin Books USA Inc.,
375 Hudson Street, New York, New York 10014 U.S.A.
Penguin Books Ltd, 27 Wrights Lane, London W8 5TZ, England
Penguin Books Australia Ltd, Ringwood, Victoria, Australia
Penguin Books Canada Ltd, 2801 John Street, Markham, Ontario, Canada L3R 1B4
Penguin Books (N.Z.) Ltd, 182–190 Wairau Road, Auckland 10, New Zealand

Penguin Books Ltd, Registered Offices: Harmondsworth, Middlesex, England

First published in 1990 by Viking Penguin, a division of Penguin Books USA Inc.
10 9 8 7 6 5 4 3 2 1
Text copyright © B.G. Hennessy, 1990
Illustrations copyright © Tracey Campbell Pearson, 1990
All rights reserved

Library of Congress Cataloging in Publication Data
Hennessy, B.G. (Barbara G.)   School days
by B.G. Hennessy ; illustrated by Tracey Campbell Pearson.   p.   cm.
Summary: Rhyming text and illustrations describe the familiar faces and objects of a day at school.
ISBN 0-670-83025-9
[1. Schools—Fiction   2. Stories in rhyme.]   I. Pearson, Tracey
Campbell, ill.   II. Title.
PZ8.3.H418Sc 1990   [E]—dc20 90-32014
Printed in Japan

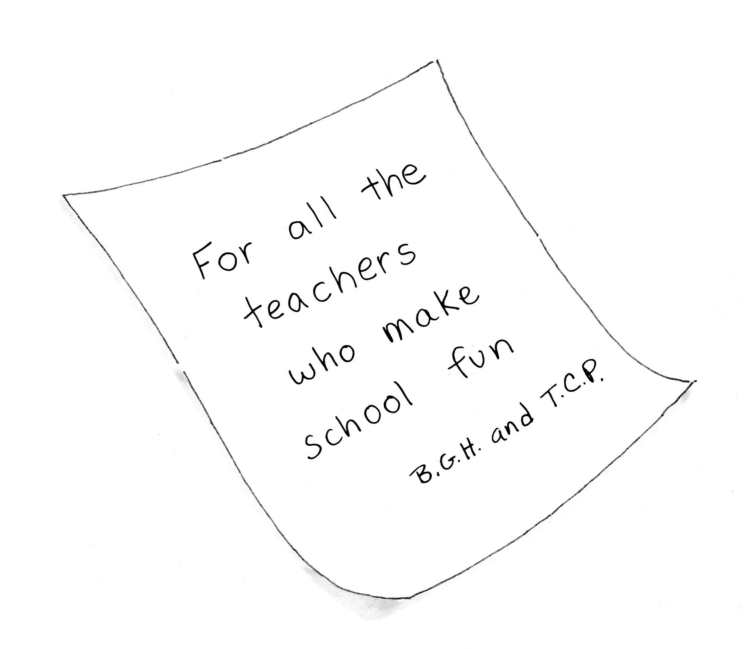

For all the teachers who make school fun

B.G.H. and T.C.P.

School bus, cubby, starting bell

Circle time, then show and tell.

Bookshelves, desks, pencil sharpener,

New friends, old friends, plant monitor.

Shapes and numbers, alphabet,
Puzzles, blocks, classroom pet.

Making rhymes and letter games,
Telling time and learning names.

Matthew, Dee, Mark and Claire,
Jason, Nancy and Pierre.

Molly, Sam and Gregory,
Ruby, Max and Hillary.

Daniel, Jill and Jennifer,
Gail, Rebecca, Christopher.

Crayons, scissors, markers, glue,

Smocks and paper, a perfect blue.

Music teacher, Librarian,

Coach and Nurse, Custodian.

Lunch box, sandwich, popcorn, juice,

Cookies, apple, Matt's front tooth!

Recess, fun time, run, jump, race,
Ball and tag, touch home base.

Feeling sad, feeling mad,
Someone has been very bad.

Seesaw, swings and sky high slides,

One more minute, one last ride.

Hearing stories, sitting still,

Listen, line up, fire drill!

Writing, reading, practicing,

Waiting for the bell to ring.

Backpack, work book, pencil case,

Everything is in its place.

Now it's time for school to end
Say goodbye to all your friends.